Bird Child

Nan Forler

Illustrated by
François Thisdale

Tundra Books

Published in Canada by Tundra Books,

75 Sherbourne Street, Toronto, Ontario M5A 2P9

Published in the United States by Tundra Books of Northern New York,

P.O. Box 1030, Plattsburgh, New York 12901

Library of Congress Control Number: 2008909725

Library and Archives Canada Cataloguing in Publication

Forler, Nan

    Bird child / Nan Forler ; illustrated by François Thisdale.

ISBN 978-0-88776-894-1

    I. Thisdale, François, 1964- II. Title.

PS8611.O76B75 2009   jC813'.6   C2008-906640-5

We acknowledge the financial support of the Government of Canada through the Book Publishing Industry Development Program (BPIDP) and that of the Government of Ontario through the Ontario Media Development Corporation's Ontario Book Initiative. We further acknowledge the support of the Canada Council for the Arts and the Ontario Arts Council for our publishing program.

ONTARIO ARTS COUNCIL
CONSEIL DES ARTS DE L'ONTARIO

Printed and bound in Canada

1 2 3 4 5 6   14 13 12 11 10 09

For my parents, who gave me wings,

for Kevin, who inspires me to fly,

and for Dillon and Maia, my sweet bird children.

– N.F.

To Nini,

Who taught me to fly.

– F.T.

Once there was a tiny girl with wobbly arms and legs, all skin and bones like a newly hatched bird. Her eyes were sharp and bright and her flyaway hair was as black as the raven that perched on the fence at the end of her drive. The tiny girl's name was Eliza.

Now, the special thing about some children is that they can skip double Dutch from one recess bell to the next; others can throw a snowball and hit a stop sign from far, far away. The special thing about Eliza was that she could fly.

When Eliza was still a baby, she and her mother would wait until her dad had gone to work, until her brother had gone to school. Then her mother would put on some music. She would wrap her strong arms around Eliza's baby-bird body and nestle her in her arms like a fragile gift. She would stroke the back of Eliza's downy head and together, with eyes closed, they would fly through dreams and love.

"Look down and see what is," her mother would tell her. "Now, look up and see what can be."

Looking down, Eliza would see fields of snow like mounds of sparkling, white sugar, a house poking through here, a tree poking through there; the yellow school bus, taking her brother to school on wet, black roads.

Looking up, she would see the bright sunlight reflecting off her wings, showing her the way. She would see a bird, gliding along, guiding her forward. And she would see herself, dancing and twirling in the feathery, white clouds.

As she grew, Eliza had days that made her feel like floating.

"How was school?" her mother would ask, as she got off the bus.

"Great!" she would exclaim, as the day overflowed and spilled from her.

Other times, Eliza would trudge down the steps of the school bus with heavy feet. On those days, Eliza's mother would take her home and nestle her in her arms once more.

"Look down and see what is," she would remind her daughter. "Now, look up and see what can be."

One day, Eliza's bus made a new stop in front of an old house. It looked as worn and tired as the clothing on the girl who burst through the door and bounded up the steps of the bus.

"I'm Lainey!" she told the bus driver and sat alone on the front seat.

Lainey had yellow hair that stuck out like straw from beneath a red woolen hat. The edges of her brown coat were feathered and frayed. The coat was torn over one shoulder in an angry snarl, letting fingers of cold creep in and scratch at her skin. The buttons on the coat were an odd collection of circles: a large blue one, then tarnished metal, brown checkered cloth, and a sparkly mauve button, so dazzling that it made the cloth around it look even more worn.

In class, the teacher gave Lainey the empty desk beside Eliza. The two girls worked silently, side by side. Eliza peeked over her shoulder and watched Lainey draw sunlight and birds and feathery white clouds and a castle that reached to the sky.

Each day, Lainey's face became more familiar, yet each day, she became more and more alone. The children teased her and yanked on her yellow straw braids. They squealed past her, playing games that she was not invited to join. Eliza watched as the sunlight and birds faded from Lainey's drawings.

In the schoolyard one day, the boy from bus stop number three swaggered over to Lainey. He snatched her red woolen hat and fired it into the wet snow.

The others kicked the snow into icy fountains, smothering her hat beneath a pile of white and cold.

The boy lifted a mitten-load of snow and smushed it into her face, wiping away what was left of the smile she'd had on her first day of school.

Eliza said nothing. She stood like a statue with her boots sinking deeper and deeper into the snow, her voice dry as a mouthful of wool, and watched it happen.

No one said a word.

Cold winter silence.

Then, the school bell.

Eliza ran to the doors, away from Lainey and her cold, wet face.

From the window, Eliza watched Lainey trudge alone through the snowdrifts. Frost nipped Lainey's ears and the wind tugged at her worn coat with its unmatched buttons. She stumbled into class, shaking and blinking away snow, trying to shiver off the day.

Lainey did not cry and she did not smile. It was as though the others had taken what was inside her and buried it along with her hat. She collapsed onto her seat and picked up her pencil. And from that girl came drawings of her sadness that made Eliza feel shame.

The next day, Lainey was not at her bus stop. The windows of her broken-down house stared blankly at Eliza. The blinds were pulled shut to keep out the roar of the school bus, the taunting voices of the children, and the brightness of the sunshine.

After school, Eliza told her mother the story of Lainey and the sad pictures she drew. She told her about the cold, wet snow and the silence that followed.

"Tell me something special about her," Eliza's mother asked.

"Well, she does beautiful artwork . . . and the mauve button on her coat sparkles in the sunshine."

Eliza's mother placed her hands on each of her daughter's shoulders. She brushed Eliza's flyaway hair off her face and looked deep into her sharp, bright eyes.

"It sounds like Lainey needs someone to help her fly."

That night, Eliza listened to her music and thought about Lainey for a very long time – until she knew what she had to do.

Just then, on the other side of town, Lainey saw a light peek through her blinds and a tiny hand reach through. She was lifted up, up out of her bed, up through her window, up into the indigo sky.

"Look down and see what is," Eliza called out, clutching Lainey's hand. "Now, look up and see what can be."

Lainey looked down as Eliza pointed out ribbons of cars curling along snowy roads and streetlamps casting warm halos of light over Lainey's house.

The two girls looked up and saw a navy blue blanket of sky with tiny pinpricks of light. The stars winked at them and seemed to become bigger and brighter as they flew.

Lainey was waiting at her bus stop the next morning. At recess, she fastened the unmatched buttons on her coat and walked outside.

The boy from stop number three raced over to her and snatched her red woolen hat. The others joined in, laughing and falling in the snow.

Eliza reached down inside herself and found her wings. She took a deep breath and called out in her biggest little voice, "Give her back her hat!"

Everyone turned and stared at the tiny, bird-like girl.

Then another voice shouted, "Yeah, give it back." Soon many voices, low and high, big and small, joined in. They stared at the boy and waited.

"Here's your dumb hat." He marched off, followed by two others. The rest remained behind and played in the fresh, new snow.

Lainey pulled her hat over her ears and began to roll a mound of snow into a ball.

"Can I play with you?" Eliza asked.

Lainey looked up from beneath her red woolen hat and smiled. And in that smile was the bright sunlight sparkling against Lainey's mauve button, showing her the way; a tiny, bird-like girl, all skin and bones, guiding her forward; and Lainey herself, dancing and twirling in the feathery, white clouds.